Saturday Popular Concerts.

DIRECTOR—Mr. S. ARTHUR CHAPPELL.

Four Hundred and Ninety-fifth Concert.*

PROGRAMME FROM THE WORKS OF

Various Masters.

SATURDAY AFTERNOON, DECEMBER 12th, 1874

QUARTET, in A, Op. 18, No. 5, for two Violins, Viola,
and Violoncello. *Beethoven.*

(Thirteenth performance at the Popular Concerts.)

Allegro—A major.
Minuetto e Trio—A major.
Andante cantabile, con variazioni—D major.
Allegro—A major.

Madame NORMAN-NÉRUDA,
Herr L. RIES, Mr. ZERBINI, and Signor PIATTI.

Though all the movements of the Quartet in A major are
beautiful, it probably owes the universal favour it has met
with from amateurs to the third movement—an *andante
cantabile*, with five variations and *coda*, founded upon a
melody as graceful as it is unpretending. The leading themes
in each movement are subjoined :—

Tenth Concert of the Seventeenth Season.

Allegro (first subject).

(Episode.)

(Second subject—in E minor.)

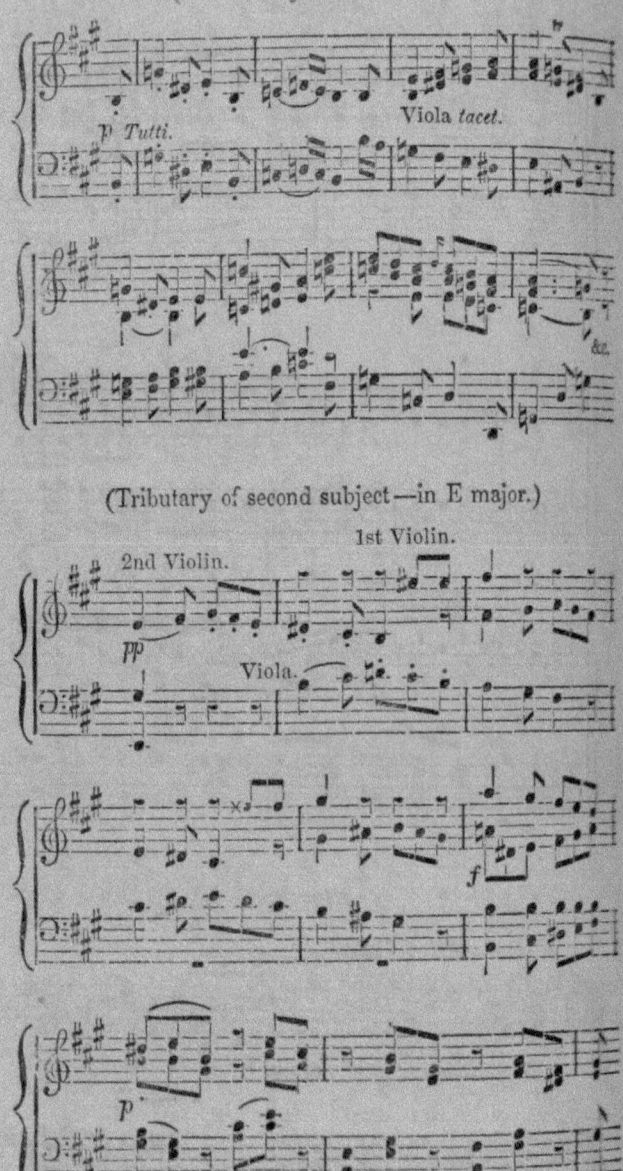

(Tributary of second subject—in E major.)

(Peroration.)

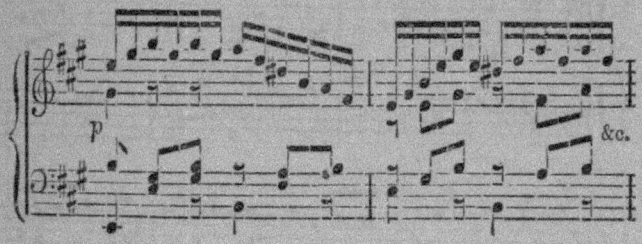

Minuetto.

1st and 2nd Violins.

Viola and Violoncello *tacent.*

Trio.

Adagio cantabile (theme).

(Variation 1.)

(Variation 2.)

(Variation 3.)

(Variation 4.)

(Variation 5.)

(Coda.)

Finale (first theme).

Second subject.

(Compare the above with the second subject in the *finale*
of the *Sonate Pathetique*, Op. 13).

The Quartet in A major is perhaps the least elaborately
constructed of the six Quartets belonging to Op. 18. It is
nevertheless, in its way, as truly a masterpiece as any of its
companions. It was first introduced by Herr Joachim, Herr
Deichmann, Mr. Doyle, and Signor Piatti, at the twelfth
concert of the first season— May 30, 1859.

SONG, Mr. SANTLEY. *Alwyn.*

(MOORE's Translation of ANACREON.)

ODE.

I pray thee, by the gods above,
Give me the mighty bowl I love,
And let me sing, in wild delight,
"I will—I will be mad to-night!"
Alcmœon once, as legends tell,
Was frenzied by the fiends of hell ;
Orestes, too, with naked tread,
Frantic pac'd the mountain-head,
And why? a murder'd mother's shade
Haunted them still where'er they strayed.
But ne'er could I a murderer be,
The grape alone shall bleed by me;
Yet I can shout, with wild delight,
"I will—I will be mad to-night!"

Alcides self, in days of yore,
Imbu'd his hands in youthful gore,
And brandish'd, with a maniac joy,
The quiver of th' expiring boy:
And Ajax, with tremendous shield,
Infuriate scorn'd the guiltless field ;
But I, whose hands no weapon ask,
No armour but this joyous flask,
The trophy of whose frantic hours
Is but a scatter'd wreath of flowers,
Ever I can sing, with wild delight,
"I will—I will be mad to-night!"

SONATA, in G major, Op. 29 (or 31), for
Pianoforte alone.*   *Beethoven.*

(Ninth performance at the Popular Concerts.)

Allegro vivace—G major.
Adagio grazioso—C major.
Rondo, allegretto, presto—G major.

Mr. CHARLES HALLÉ.

This sonata is the first of the three very remarkable works (the
other two being in D minor and E flat major) which, in some
editions, are marked Op. 29, in others, Op. 31. Liszt, Lenz, and
Thayer, adopt the latter nomenclature, and are most probably
correct, the stringed instrument quintet in C major being the
genuine "Op. 29." The three sonatas, Op. 31, were composed in
1802, or 1803, dedicated to the Comtesse de Browne (to whom
were also inscribed the three sonatas, Op. 10), and purchased by
Nägali, a music publisher at Zurich, who brought them out,
full of engraver's errors, which exasperated Beethoven beyond
measure. Between the date of their composition and that of
the sonata in D, Op 28 (*Pastorale*), Beethoven produced,
besides several works of less importance, the three sonatas
for pianoforte and violin, dedicated to the Emperor Alexander (Op. 30). Op. 31 is the last in which three grand
sonatas appear as one work. Beethoven has bequeathed to
us no less than ten of such rich legacies—viz. the three trios
(with piano), Op. 1; three sonatas (solo), Op. 2; ditto, ditto
(ditto), Op. 10; ditto, ditto (ditto), Op. 31; three sonatas
for piano and violin, Op. 12; ditto, ditto (ditto), Op. 30;
three trios for stringed instruments, Op. 9; three string
quartets, Op 59, (Razoumowski); and the six string quartets,
Op. 18, which first appeared in sets of three each. The
Sonata in G major is pure Beethoven from end to end, notwithstanding a certain quasi-plagiarism from Haydn, in the
middle movement. The vigour of the leading theme, which
gives tone to the first *allegro*, emphatically proclaims the
independent spirit in which the composer sat down to write,

---

* No. 16 of Beethoven's Sonatas, edited by Mr. CHARLES HALLÉ
—published by CHAPPELL and Co. 50, New Bond Street.
+ *The Chronologisches Verzeichniss* of Mr. A. W. Thayer gives an
account of various editions of these sonatas. The author, however,
says nothing about the dedication.

and the new train of thought that was invading his prolific brain :—

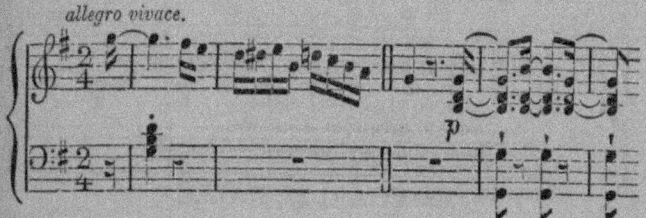

No sooner is the passage to the dominant effected, than the following transition startles the ear :—

Once again in G, we have a brilliant development, in unison, of that feature of the leading subject which is contained in its second bar :—

The theme is then repeated in G ; and now, instead of the progression to the dominant of the leading key, we have a progression to F sharp, dominant of B :—

—in which last-named key Beethoven introduces, without preamble, the second subject (melody only quoted) :—

After eight bars in the major key, the theme is given in the minor, to the left hand :—

Theme in B minor.

This alternation of major and minor is a striking characteristic of the second subject. Of the development, the subjoined is a prominent feature :—

—further on, deriving fresh interest from a wholly new treatment :—

When the foregoing is worked up to a full cadence in the key of the second subject (B), we have a tributary, in which the coquetting between the major and minor (the minor now taking the lead) receives further illustration :—

With eight bars of this the first part is brought to a close in B minor, the first theme being then immediately resumed in G major

After the "repetition," we are introduced to the second part, precisely in the same manner. The elaborations are constructed exclusively upon the most conspicuous features of the leading theme. First, there is a progression to C minor :—

Then a series of interesting modulations (employed upon the same material) lead to B flat major, in which the brilliant unison passage is referred to :—

This is now interrupted by a wholly new idea, in the form of an episode, with which it speedily amalgamates :—

Episode.

Short work, however, is made of this, the episode being only allowed to speak twice—once in C minor and once in D minor. From the latter, through G minor, we got back to the dominant of the original key, upon which the composer has built one of his favourite pedal points, more lengthy and tantalising than usual. This, commencing brilliantly—to keep colour with what immediately leads to it :—

—ultimately subsides into a calmer strain, finishing off with the subjoined period, in which the obstinate reiteration of the flat ninth (E flat) against the pedal note (D) is peculiar to Beethoven* :—

* See the rondo of the Grand Sonata in C, dedicated to Count Waldstein (Op. 53).

After a long suspense, the first subject re-enters with vigour :—

First subject.

The curtailment of this part of the movement here is as masterly as (with a view to the subsequent *coda*, where the old materials are again brought into request) it is well-judged. The progression to the dominant (D) is immediately succeeded by a modulation to the dominant of E (B) :—

—in which key (with the alternations between major and minor already noted) the second subject reappears. The primary key of the *Allegro*, however, being G, it was impossible to remain very long in E at this point of the movement; and Beethoven, never at a loss, avails himself of the change to the minor to get back to G major, in a bold and striking manner :—

Second theme in E minor.   Interrupted.

3 H

We have then in the new key, a recapitulation of the first part, terminating, as before, with the tributary, in which G minor and major are now coquetted with, as B minor and major were in the first instance :—

The *coda*, which sets out with a reference to the leading theme, terminates with an entirely new feature :—

It was here—between the third and fourth bars—that the interpolated passage originally appeared (in the edition of Nägali, a music-publisher at Zurich, to whom the sonatas had been sold), which so enraged Beethoven, when his pupil, Ries, was reading over the proof sheets, in the composer's presence :—

[The interpolator was probably Nägali himself, or some Zurich professor, in his confidence, who did not appreciate Beethoven's rhythmical independence. Some editions—and among others that of M. Moscheles—perpetuated the error.] The further development of this graceful episode brings the *Allegro* to an end.

The *Adagio*, appropriately styled "*grazioso*," is one of the longest, most beautiful, and—notwithstanding the resemblance between the opening of the leading theme and an air from Haydn's *Creation* ("In native worth")—one of the most original in all the sonatas of Beethoven. Thus, with the ample melodic phraseology of the most refined Italian *cantilena*, it begins :—

The accompaniment, in triplets, is too simple to need quoting. The manner in which this engaging melody is embellished, at each successive recurrence, will make an impression on attentive hearers, without the aid of quotation. After being presented a second time, *in extenso* (adorned with brilliant *fioriture*), modulating to the dominant, it makes way for the second subject :—

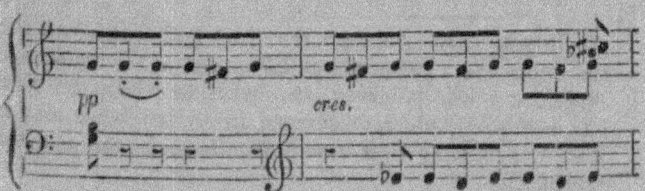

This impressive theme is wound up by a *ritornelle*, beginning as subjoined :—

—and to which allusion is subsequently made, with increased effect. A brilliant cadenza (*ad libitum*), succeeding to a pause, then reintroduces the principal subject, after a repetition of which—with fresh embellishments—a long and interesting episode sets out in the minor key of C :—

—and is continued in such a manner as to render it more and more attractive :—

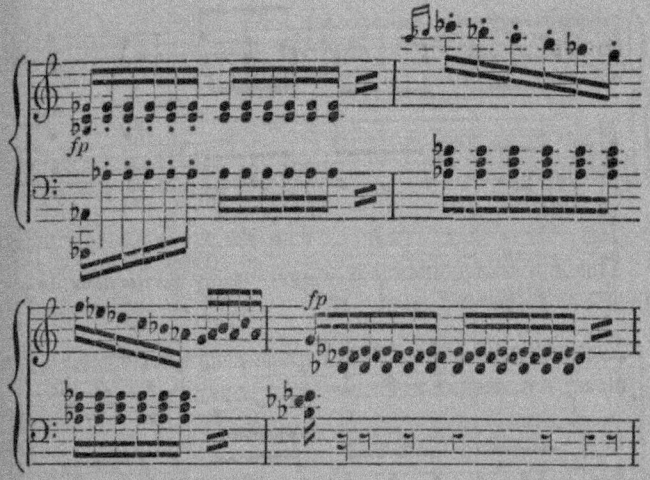

This episode — together with the richly harmonized *codetta* :—

—the bridge over which we are made to pass once more to the principal subject—is perhaps the most impressive part of the *Adagio*. The leading theme makes its reappearance in a new dress :—

—and is given twice, *in extenso* (as before), more brightly decked out as it progresses, like the wife of Geraint, in the Laureate's *Idylls of the King*. The second subject is reintroduced almost precisely in the same manner as before, and in the same key (see page 214), but considerably modified and extended. The *ritornelle*, also modified and extended, follows in due course, and is succeeded by a still more florid one brilliant *cadenza*, leading to a fresh apparition of the never unwelcome leading theme. We have then a *coda*, growing naturally out of the principal subject :—

—which, developed at considerable length, terminates a slow movement, unique in its kind :—

Long as is this *Adagio*, it never becomes prolix, such is the variety and skill with which it is conducted.

There is no *minuetto*, or *scherzo*, in this sonata. The *Rondo* is in keeping with the rest, though in strong contrast with the first *Allegro*. Nothing can be more graceful than its leading subject :—

This is submitted, in the course of the movement, to several ingenious transformations — as, first, for example, when it is allotted to the left hand, with an accompaniment in triplets for the right :—

—which in the progress of development, becomes almost as melodious as the theme itself. The second subject (in the dominant) partakes of the individuality of the first transformation of its companion :—

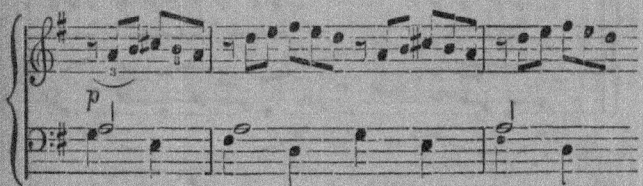

This, worked out, conducts us once again—after a brilliant peroration, in which the triplet motion is incessantly kept up —to the principal theme, now supported by an entirely new bass, marked by the vigour for which Beethoven is so frequently noticeable, and which (like certain passages in Mozart's quartets) would no doubt have been reprehended by the pedants :—

A recurrence of the first transformation now ensues (the subject given to the left hand, with triplet passages for the right)—but this time in the minor key, and leading to a sort of *free fantasia,* in canon on the octave, " *con alcune licenzie* "

—as was generally the practice of Beethoven, when calling in the temporary aid of certain contrapuntal devices :—

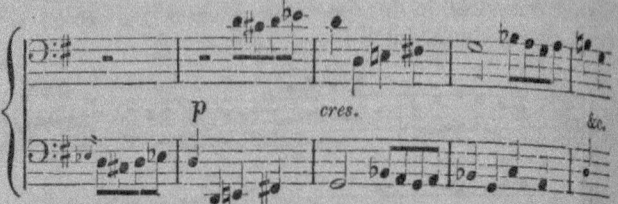

This *"free fantasia"* culminating in E flat, is for an instant arrested by a remarkably bold episode :—

—with which, however, it soon makes " common accord," the two pursuing their course together through a series of modulations, the interest of which is sustained with singular effect.

The dominant close being reached at last, the leading theme (with the triplets still at work) comes back unexpectedly, and in a fresh disguise :—

We have then a " recapitulation " (triplets never ceasing), which comprises, in due form, the return of the second subject, now in the key of G :—

—with a repetition, in the usual style, of all the first matter. No modification calls for particular notice, until we arrive at the *coda*, which sets out, on a dominant *pedale*, with a new treatment of the second section of the leading theme :—

A noticeable point in this *coda* occurs where the theme is, as it were, divided into halves—the first half *allegretto* :—

—the second half *adagio* :—

The *adagio* eventually gives way to a *presto* :—

—which *presto*, as animated as anything else in the *Rondo*, terminates, in a thoroughly characteristic manner, one of the most original sonatas invented by the inexhaustible genius of Beethoven. The last bars :—

—subsiding gradually from *fortissimo* to *pianissimo*—suggest the gradual fading away of a vivid and absorbing dream.

The Sonata in G major was first introduced by Mr. Charles Hallé, at the nineteenth concert of the fourth season. —April 28, 1862.

AIR, Mr. SANTLEY.   *Handel.*

Revenge! revenge! Timotheus cries!
  See the furies arise,
  See the snakes that they rear,
  How they hiss in their hair,
And the sparkles that flash in their eyes!
  Behold a ghastly band,
  Each a torch in his hand!
Those are Grecian ghosts that in battle were slain,
  And, unburied, remain
  Inglorious on the plain.

From the well-known *cantata* set to Dryden's Ode, *Alexander's Feast, or the Power of Music,* first presented on February 19, 1736, "after the manner of an oratorio—that is to say, without action." Of this performance, the following account is rendered in *The London Daily Press* of the day:

"There never was, upon the like occasion, so numerous and splendid an audience at any theatre in London, there being at least thirteen hundred persons present; and it is judged that the receipts of the house could not amount to less than £450. The new composition met with general applause, though attended with the inconvenience of having the performers placed at too great a distance from the audience, which we hear will be rectified the next time of performance."

** Mr. CHARLES HALLÉ will perform on one of Messrs. JOHN BROADWOOD and SONS' Concert Grand Pianofortes.

———

TRIO, in B flat, Op. 99, No. 1, for Pianoforte, Violin,
and Violoncello.   *Schubert.*

(Seventeenth performance at the Popular Concerts.)

Allegro moderato—B flat major.
Andante un poco mosso—E flat major.
Scherzo, allegro—B flat major; with Trio—E flat major.
Rondo, allegro vivace—B flat major.

Mr. CHARLES HALLÉ,
Madame NORMAN-NÉRUDA, and Signor PIATTI.

"One glance at this trio, and all the pitiful clouds of life
disperse, and the world shines again as fresh and bright as
ever. It is now some ten years since the first Schubert trio
made its appearance, like a fiery messenger from the skies,
and scattered all the petty musical troubles of the day. It
was exactly his hundredth work, and very shortly after its
publication, on the 19th November, 1828, he died. The
newly published one appears to be the earlier in date of composition, but it bears no marks of earlier style, and was probably written only shortly before the other — the well-
known one in E flat (Op. 100). Internally, however, they
differ essentially. The first movement *there* was full of stern
wrath and infinite regrets: *here* it is graceful, confiding, and
girlish. The adagio in *that* was one long sigh, and enough
for a breaking heart: in *this* it is a happy dream, waving its
wings in the varying current of sweet human feeling. The
scherzos are much alike, but I give the preference to that in
the E flat trio. On the last movements I withhold my judg-
ment. In short, the E flat trio is busy, masculine, dramatic:
the B flat, sorrowful, lyrical, feminine. The new work is
indeed a precious legacy. Many and beautiful as are the
things which time brings forth, it will be long ere it produces
another Schubert." Thus writes Schumann (*Gesammelte
Schriften*, vol i, p. 302). Elsewhere (in a review of the
last sonatas), speaking of the E flat Trio, Schumann says:—
"As for me, it has always seemed as Schubert's last work,
and his most individual and original piece·" Schumann had
not then made acquaintance with the symphony in C.

Allegro moderato (first theme).

Violoncello in octaves with Violin.

Cello. &c.

Andante un poco mosso.

pp Violoncello.

pp Pianoforte.

Scherzo.

p Pianoforte.

Trio.

Finale.

In the recently published *Life of Schubert*, by Herr Kreissle von Hellborn a few particulars are given about the trios—Schubert's only compositions of this class. That in B flat was composed in 1826, and is numbered Op. 99. That in E flat (Op 100) was composed in November, 1827, and published in the following year. The autograph MS. is in the hands of the Countess Rosa von Almafy, at Vienna. Herr Brahms is possessor of the composer's original sketch. "These two trios," says Herr Kreissle, "were among the few of Schubert's instrumental works that had the good fortune to be played during his lifetime, in public or private, by musicians attached to the composer, and able to do them justice; and they were received with great applause whenever performed. They were often played by Boclet, at the piano, Schuppanzigh (Beethoven's Schuppanzigh), at the violin, and Linke, at the violoncello. Boclet was enthusiastic for Schubert; and at one of their meetings, in the house of Spaun, he knelt and kissed the hand of his hero, calling out to the company at the same time, that they did not know "what a treasure they possessed in Schubert."

The Trio in B flat was first introduced by Herr Pauer, Herr Joachim, and Signor Piatti, at the 21st concert of the fourth season—May 19, 1862.

END OF THE FOUR HUNDRED AND NINETY-FIFTH CONCERT.

J. MALLETT, PRINTER, 59, WARDOUR STREET, SOHO. W.

MONDAY POPULAR CONCERTS.

MONDAY EVENING, DECEMBER 14th, 1874.

PROGRAMME.

PART I.

QUARTET, in B flat, No. 9, for two Violins, Viola, and
Violoncello.. *Mozart.*

Madame NORMAN-NÉRUDA,
MM. L. RIES, ZERBINI, and PIATTI.

RECIT, "Deeper, and deeper still." }
AIR, "Waft her, angels." } ....*Handel.*

Mr. SIMS REEVES.

NOCTURNE, in E major, No. 18, }
BARCAROLLE, in F sharp major, } for Pianoforte alone ...... *Chopin.*

Mr. CHARLES HALLÉ.

PART II.

SONATA DA CAMERA, in G minor, for Violin, with
Pianoforte Accompaniment .... *Locatelli.*

(First time at the Popular Concerts.)
Madame NORMAN-NÉRUDA.

SONG, "Ave Maria."..*Schubert.*

Mr. SIMS REEVES.

SONATA, in A, Op. 47 (dedicated to Kreutzer), for Pianoforte
and Violin .... *Beethoven.*

(By desire.)
Mr. CHARLES HALLÉ and Madame NORMAN-NÉRUDA.

Conductor - - Mr. ZERBINI.

3 K